D0606624

CLARK THE SHARK
LOVES CHRISTMAS

WRITTEN BY **BRUCE HALE**   ILLUSTRATED BY **GUY FRANCIS**

WITHDRAWN

HARPER
An Imprint of HarperCollinsPublishers

To Ronna Zigmand and the cool kids of New Delhi's American Embassy School
—B.H.

To Shane Rowley
—G.F.

Clark the Shark Loves Christmas
Copyright © 2016 by HarperCollins Publishers
All rights reserved. Manufactured in China.
No part of this book may be used or reproduced in any manner whatsoever without
written permission except in the case of brief quotations embodied in critical articles
and reviews. For information address HarperCollins Children's Books, a division of
HarperCollins Publishers, 195 Broadway, New York, NY 10007.
www.harpercollinschildrens.com
Library of Congress Control Number: 2016936319
ISBN 978-0-06-237452-3
The artist used acrylic to create the illustrations for this book.
Typography by Victor Joseph Ochoa
16 17 18 19 20 SCP 10 9 8 7 6 5 4 3 2 1
❖
First Edition

It was Christmastime at Theodore Roosterfish Elementary, and all the fish were in a flurry. But no one was more excited than Clark the Shark.

"Christmas ROCKS!" Clark yelled. "I LOVE the decorations!"

"And the COOKIES are even BETTER!" he cried.

"But the caroling is the BEST!" he yodeled.
"FA-LA-LA-LA-LAAA!"

"Cool your jets, Clark," said his friend Joey Mackerel. "The best part of Christmas isn't munching and crunching and singing too loud."

"What do you mean?" asked Clark.

"It's . . . hard to explain," said Joey.

Then Mrs. Inkydink announced, "Time for Secret Santa!"

"*Secret* Santa?" said Clark. "I didn't know Santa was a spy. Cool!"

Mrs. Inkydink explained that everyone would pick a name from a hat, and whichever name you drew, you'd get that classmate a gift. "But you can't tell who you picked," she said.

"Where does the spying come in?" Clark wondered.

Everyone picked names. Clark chose Benny
Blowfish. But all he wanted to know was . . .
"Who picked my name?"
Nobody spoke.
"It's a secret," said Mrs. Inkydink.
"I HATE secrets," said Clark.

Then Clark had a sharky idea. He told Joey,
"*Now* I get it: The best part of Christmas is
getting *presents*. So what are you giving me?"
But Joey just shook his head.

Over the next few days, Clark tried to spy like
Santa. He peeked into his classmates' desks to figure
out who had his present . . .

. . . but all he found was a shell, a sand dollar, and
an old peanut-butter-and-jellyfish sandwich.

He tried to trick his friends with rhymes like "Every fire has a spark; I bought a gift and it's for ..."

But nobody confessed. Secret Santa stayed top secret.

One morning, Mrs. Inkydink told the class, "Today is your last chance to buy a gift, because tomorrow is Secret Santa day!"

"Oh boy!" said Joey.

"Oh joy!" said Amanda Eelwiggle.

"Oh no!" cried Clark. He'd tried so hard to learn what his Secret Santa was getting him, he'd forgotten about Benny's present.

Even worse, he'd blown his allowance on the newest issue of *Captain Suckermouth*. Could Clark just give his favorite comic book to Benny?

The next morning, everyone placed their presents around the class Christmas tree. There were big gifts and small gifts, lumpy gifts and thumpy gifts. But which one was Clark's?

One by one, kids claimed their presents.

"A Hula-Hoop?" said Amanda.
"Perfect! I love to wiggle!"

"A baseball cap?" said Billy-Ray
Ray. "Someone really knows me!"

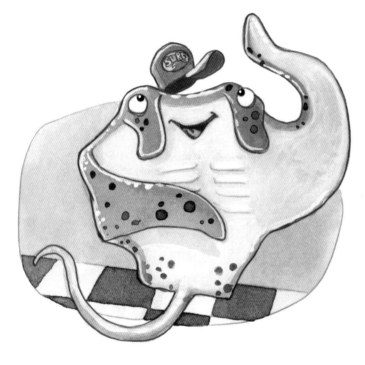

"Socks?" said Sid the Squid.
"Thank you, Secret Santa!"

Clark looked around at his smiling classmates with their perfect gifts, and his tummy gave a twinge. He should have gotten a kazoo. Did Benny even like comics?

Clark whispered to Mrs. Inkydink, "I have a problem."

"What is it?" she asked.

"All the other Secret Santas got the right gift for the right person," he said. "I'm afraid mine's not so hot."

Mrs. Inkydink patted his cheek. "It's the thought that counts."

Clark cringed. He'd been thinking only of himself.

At last it was Benny's turn. He ripped open the wrapping while Clark held his breath.

"Wow, *Captain Suckermouth*?" said Benny. "I love *Captain Suckermouth*! Thank you, Secret Santa!"

Clark was so relieved, he blurted, "You're welcome!"
Everybody laughed. "Well, so much for that secret," said Mrs. Inkydink.

Then Clark got a sweet surprise when he unwrapped his own present.

"Secret Santa's been spying on *me*!" he cried.

"Yes, he has." Benny grinned.

When all the gifts had been opened, Clark's class continued its party with cookies and carols and Christmas-y fun.

"Christmas rocks!" said Clark. "But one thing about Christmas rocks most of all."

"What's that?" asked Joey.

Clark the Shark smiled. "If you want to be smart, always give from the heart!"